BRACHIOSAURUS

A Buddy Book
by
Michael P. Goecke

ABDO
Publishing Company

VISIT US AT
www.abdopub.com

Published by ABDO Publishing Company, 4940 Viking Drive, Edina, Minnesota 55435. Copyright © 2002 by Abdo Consulting Group, Inc. International copyrights reserved in all countries. No part of this book may be reproduced in any form without written permission from the publisher.

Printed in the United States.

Edited by: Christy DeVillier
Contributing editor: Matt Ray
Graphic Design: Denise Esner, Maria Hosley
Cover Art: Denise Esner, title page
Interior Photos/Illustrations: page 4: Oil painting by Josef Moravec; pages 7, 9 & 25: Deborah Coldiron; page 15: Denise Esner; page 19: ©Douglas Henderson from *Dinosaurs, A Global View*, published by Dragon's World; page 23: John Sibbick; page 27: Corbis.

Library of Congress Cataloging-in-Publication Data

Goecke, Michael P., 1968-
  Brachiosaurus/Michael P. Goecke.
    p. cm. – (Dinosaurs set II)
    Includes index.
    Summary: Describes the physical characteristics and behavior of the large dinosaur Brachiosaurus.
    ISBN 1-57765-632-6
    1. Brachiosaurus—Juvenile literature. [1. Brachiosaurus. 2. Dinosaurs.] I. Title.

QE862.S3 G62 2002
567.914—dc21

2001027929

TABLE OF CONTENTS

What Were They? 4

How Did They Move? 6

Why Was It Special? 8

Land Of The Brachiosaurus 10

The Family Tree 14

Who Else Lived There? 18

What Did They Eat? 20

Who Were Their Enemies? 22

Family Life 24

Discovery 26

Where Are They Today? 28

Fun Dinosaur Web Sites 30

Important Words 31

Index 32

WHAT WERE THEY?

The Brachiosaurus was a huge, plant-eating dinosaur. It is one of the biggest animals ever.

Brachiosaurus
BRACK-ee-uh-SAW-rus

The Brachiosaurus was 82 feet (25 m) long. It stood about 50 feet (15 m) tall. That is as tall as three giraffes on top of each other.

The Brachiosaurus weighed about 130,000 pounds (58,967 kg). That is as heavy as 13 elephants.

How Did They Move?

The Brachiosaurus walked on four legs. Its front legs were longer than its back legs. So, the Brachiosaurus stood like a giraffe.

The Brachiosaurus had narrow feet. It was not a fast runner. The Brachiosaurus probably did not run very much.

The Brachiosaurus had a thick tail. It may have used this tail like a fifth leg. Maybe the Brachiosaurus's thick tail held up its back end.

WHY WAS IT SPECIAL?

The Brachiosaurus had a long neck. This neck was about 20 feet (6 m) long. The tall Brachiosaurus could reach food high in the trees.

The Brachiosaurus may have had a large heart. Why? A big, strong heart could move blood up its long neck.

The Brachiosaurus

LAND OF THE BRACHIOSAURUS

People have found Brachiosaurus fossils at Grand River Valley in Colorado. People have found Brachiosaurus fossils in Tanzania, Africa, too. This tells us that the Brachiosaurus lived in North America and Africa.

The Brachiosaurus lived in North America and Africa. North America and Africa are two continents. A continent is a large land mass.

The Brachiosaurus lived about 150 million years ago. That was during the late Jurassic period. The Rocky Mountains were new at this time. Rivers flowed from these mountains to a flat land. We call this land a floodplain. The Brachiosaurus lived on this flood plain. This land filled with water during rainy times. Other times, it was dry.

Rocky Mountains today

THE FAMILY TREE

The Brachiosaurus was a sauropod dinosaur. Sauropods had long necks and tails. Another sauropod dinosaur is the Camarasaurus.

The Camarasaurus was a lot like the Brachiosaurus. These sauropods lived at the same time. They looked alike. Yet, the Camarasaurus was smaller than the Brachiosaurus. The Camarasaurus was only 60 feet (18 m) long.

The Brachiosaurus had other sauropod neighbors. Two of these "long-necks" were the Apatosaurus and the Diplodocus. They lived in great herds, or groups.

WHO ELSE LIVED THERE?

One tiny, meat-eating neighbor was the Ornitholestes. This dinosaur was about five feet (two m) tall. The Ornitholestes may have eaten Brachiosaurus eggs.

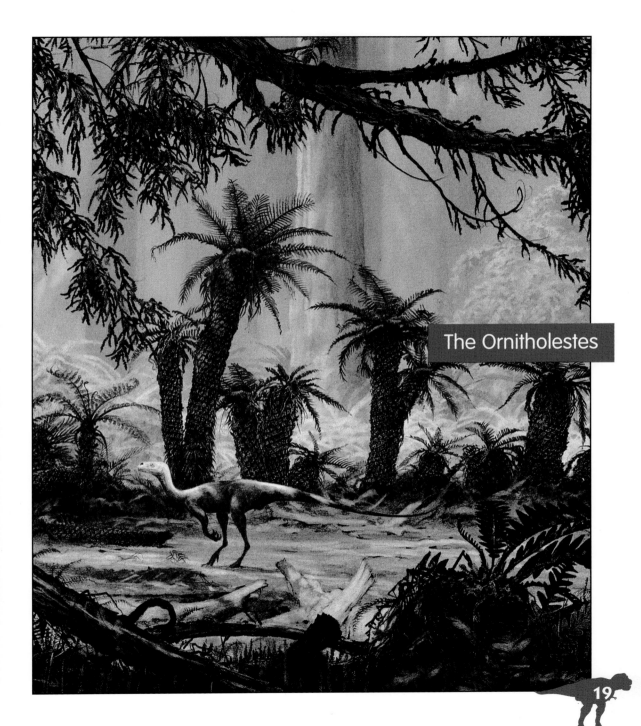

What Did They Eat?

The Brachiosaurus ate plants with its special teeth. These teeth were shaped like pegs. The Brachiosaurus tugged at leaves with these peg-like teeth. It did not chew. Instead, this large plant-eater swallowed the leaves whole.

A forest of conifer trees.

What kind of leaves did the Brachiosaurus eat? Maybe this plant-eater ate from conifer trees. Many of today's evergreen trees are conifers. Evergreen trees stay green all year long.

WHO WERE THEIR ENEMIES?

The Allosaurus was the meanest meat-eater in the late Jurassic period. Yet, the Allosaurus was much smaller than the Brachiosaurus. The Allosaurus was only 17 feet (5 m) tall. So, one Allosaurus could not kill the giant Brachiosaurus. It would take a group of Allosaurus dinosaurs to do this.

The Brachiosaurus was much bigger than the Allosaurus.

FAMILY LIFE

The Brachiosaurus probably did not raise its young. Paleontologists think it laid eggs and left. These eggs were probably as big as footballs. Maybe the giant Brachiosaurus was too big to care for its babies.

Brachiosaurus dinosaurs hatched from eggs.

Discovery

One day in 1899, a dentist in Colorado saw something strange. He saw dinosaur bones in a hill. So, the dentist showed these bones to Elmer Samuel Riggs. Elmer Riggs was a paleontologist.

Elmer Riggs had not seen dinosaur bones like these before. Riggs had discovered the first Brachiosaurus fossils.

Dinosaur bones are fossils.

27

Where Are They Today?

Smithsonian National Museum of Natural History
10th Street and Constitution Avenue
Washington, D.C. 20560
www.nmnh.si.edu/paleo/dino

Dinosaur Farm Museum
Military Road
Near Brightstone, Isle of Wight PO30 4PG
www.wightonline.co.uk/dinosaurfarm

Field Museum of Natural History
Lake Shore Drive at Roosevelt Road
Chicago, IL 60605
www.fmnh.org

BRACHIOSAURUS

NAME MEANS	Arm Lizard
DIET	Plants
WEIGHT	100,000-160,000 pounds (45,359-72,575 kg)
HEIGHT	50 feet (15 m)
TIME	Late Jurassic Period
ANOTHER SAUROPOD	Camarasaurus
SPECIAL FEATURE	Long neck
FOSSILS FOUND	USA—Colorado Tanzania—Africa

The Brachiosaurs lived 156 million years ago.

First humans appeared 1.6 million years ago.

Triassic Period	Jurassic Period	Cretaceous Period	Tertiary Period
245 Million years ago	208 Million years ago	144 Million years ago	65 Million years ago

Mesozoic Era — Cenozoic Era

29

Fun Dinosaur Web Sites

Dinosaurs
www.cfsd.k12.az.us/~tchrpg/Claudia/Diplo.html
Basic information about the Brachiosaurus, including what it looked like, and activities for children.

BBC Online – Walking with Dinosaurs
www.bbc.co.uk/dinosaurs/sci_focus/production2.shtml
From the Discovery Channel series, "Walking with Dinosaurs," learn about the size and eating habits of the Brachiosaurus.

Enchanted Learning.com
www.enchantedlearning.com/subject/dinosaurs/dinos/Brachiosaurus.shtml
Read how Brachiosaurus compares in size to other animals of today and more.

IMPORTANT WORDS

conifer trees that have needles instead of leaves. Conifers stay green all year long.

dinosaur reptiles that lived on land 248-65 million years ago.

floodplain flat land that sometimes floods with water.

fossil remains of very old animals and plants.

Jurassic period a period of time that happened 208-146 million years ago.

paleontologist someone who studies very old life (like dinosaurs), mostly by studying fossils.

sauropod a kind of dinosaur that has a long neck, a long tail, and a small head.

INDEX

Africa, **10, 11, 29**

Allosaurus, **22, 23**

Apatosaurus, **16, 17**

Camarasaurus, **14-17, 29**

Colorado, **10, 26, 29**

conifer, **21**

continent, **11**

Diplodocus, **16, 17**

eggs, **18, 24, 25**

floodplain, **12**

fossil, **10, 26, 27, 29**

Grand River Valley, Colorado, **10**

Jurassic period, **12, 22, 29**

North America, **10, 11**

Ornitholestes, **18, 19**

paleontologist, **24, 26**

Riggs, Elmer Samuel, **26**

Rocky Mountains, **12, 13**

sauropod, **14, 16, 17, 29**

Tanzania, Africa, **10, 29**